bubbles

KIT CHASE

G. P. Putnam's Sons

To my best friend, Adam,

for making each day a happy adventure

G. P. PUTNAM'S SONS
an imprint of Penguin Random House LLC
375 Hudson Street
New York, NY 10014

Library of Congress Cataloging-in-Publication Data is available upon request.

Manufactured in China by RR Donnelley Asia Printing Solutions Ltd.
ISBN 9780399545740
1 3 5 7 9 10 8 6 4 2

Design by Marikka Tamura.
Text set in LTC Powell.
The art was done in watercolor with pen and ink.

Kangaroo loved to blow bubbles.

One day, she saw some mysterious bubbles.

So she followed the bubble trail . . .

and found Koala.

"Hullo!" said Kangaroo.

Koala didn't say hello.

Koala climbed a tree instead.

"Hullo!" Kangaroo called.

Koala still didn't
say a word.

Kangaroo took a lollipop
out of her pocket.

Koala didn't want it.

She took out a pinwheel.

Koala didn't want that either.

"Bother," said Kangaroo, slowly walking away.

Kangaroo sat down to think and blow bubbles.

Soon, some bubbles floated by again.

Kangaroo and Koala blew friendly bubbles to each other.

They blew small bubbles

and big bubbles,

crocodile bubbles

and tiger bubbles.

It was a happy bubble party.

Suddenly, the bubbles
began to stick together,

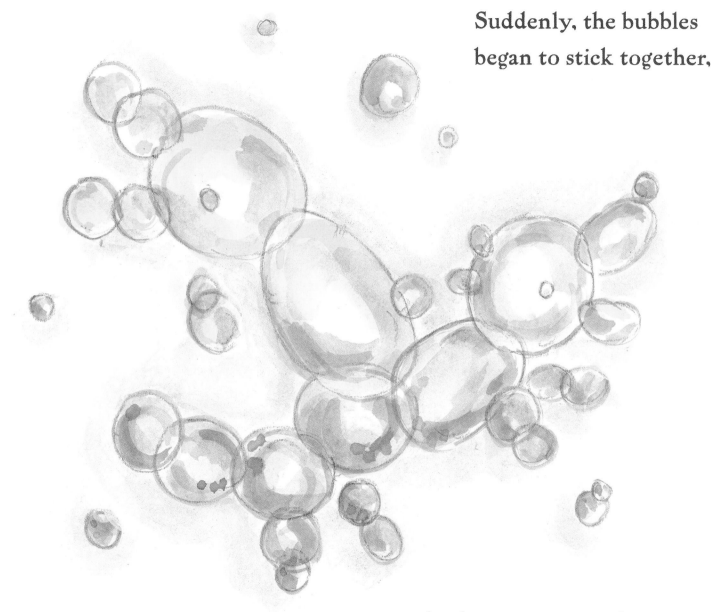

and they grew bigger,

and bigger,

and even bigger!

The bubbles had turned into a great big

bubble monster!

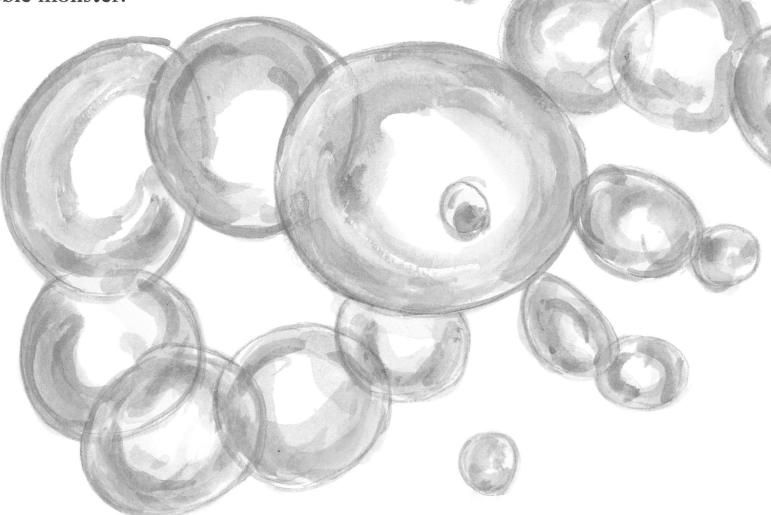

And it was heading right toward Kangaroo!

"Yikes!" squawked Koala.

"Help!" squealed Kangaroo.

All of a sudden,
Koala felt brave.

"Let's go get that bubble
monster!" said Koala.

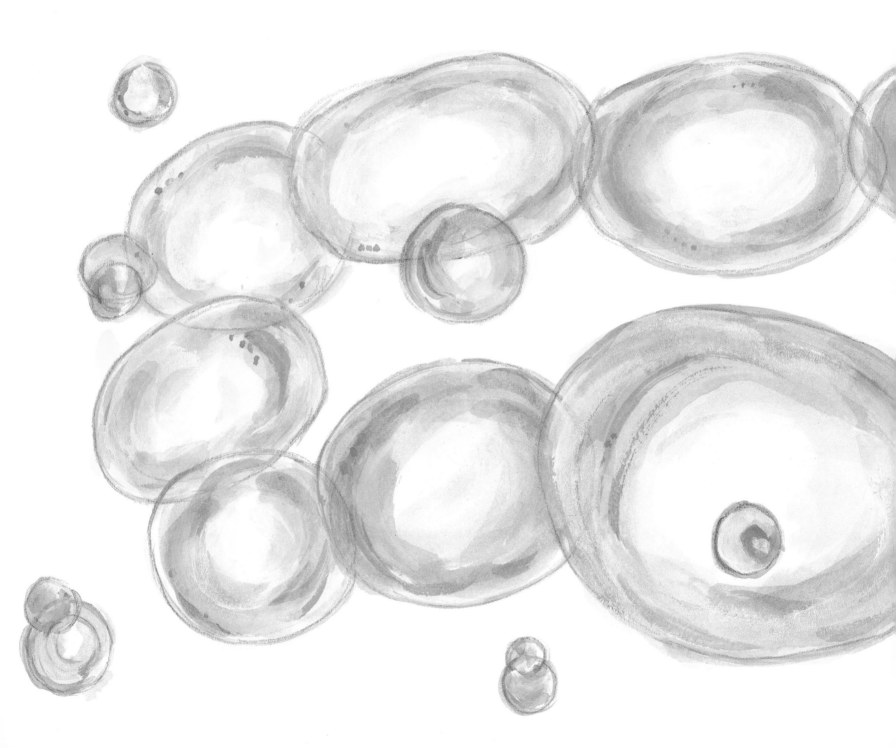

Kangaroo and Koala looked around.
The bubble monster was gone.

"Hullo," said Kangaroo.

"Hello!" said Koala.

Kangaroo had bubble gum in her pocket.

And they blew bubbles happily ever after.